SWITCH ON
A LIGHT

SWITCH ON A LIGHT

Joy Richardson

Illustrated by
Sue Barclay and Dee McLean

Hamish Hamilton · London

The author and publishers would like to
thank Robert Gwynne B.Sc. for his help
and advice in the preparation of this book.

351751z
J·537

HAMISH HAMILTON CHILDREN'S BOOKS

Penguin Books Ltd, 27 Wrights Lane, London W8 5TZ (Publishing & Editorial)
and Harmondsworth, Middlesex, England (Distribution & Warehouse)
Viking Penguin Inc., 40 West 23rd Street, New York, New York 10010, U.S.A.
Penguin Books Australia Ltd, Ringwood, Victoria, Australia
Penguin Books Canada Ltd, 2801 John Street, Markham, Ontario, Canada L3R 1B4
Penguin Books (N.Z.) Ltd, 182–190 Wairau Road, Auckland 10, New Zealand

First published in Great Britain 1988 by
Hamish Hamilton Children's Books
Text Copyright © 1988 by Joy Richardson
Illustrations Copyright © 1988 by Sue Barclay and (activities) Dee McLean
Design by Monica Chia

British Library Cataloguing-in-Publication Data:
Richardson, Joy
Switch on a light. – (Science seekers).
1. Light – J Juvenile literature
I. Title II. Series
535   QC360
ISBN 0–241–12087–X

Printed in Belgium

CONTENTS

If there is not enough sunlight to see by, you can make up for it by turning on an electric light.

When you push the light switch, the room brightens up as if by magic.

Where does the light come from?

You can begin to find out by looking carefully at the lights around your house.

But ELECTRICITY IS DANGEROUS. You must never play with things connected to the electricity supply in your house.

You can find out a lot about how lights work by using:

BATTERIES which will push a small electric current safely round a thin wire.

Single-strand plastic-coated WIRE.

TORCH BULBS which you can screw into little plastic BULB-HOLDERS.

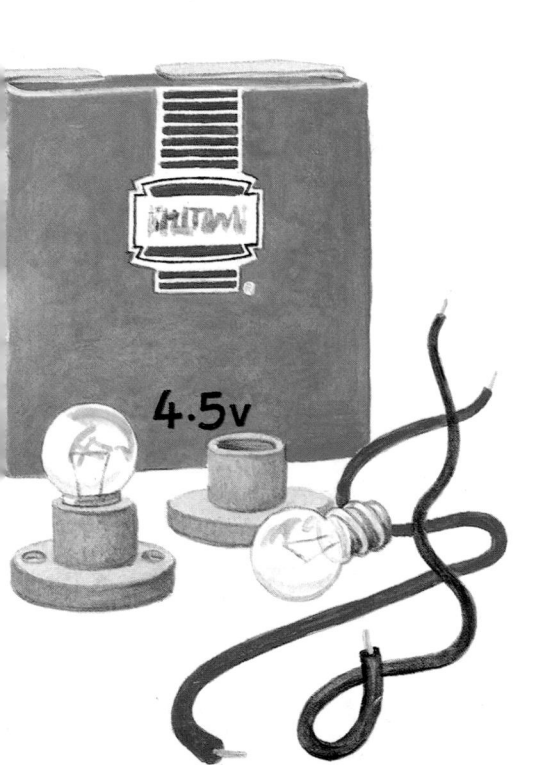

4·5v

7

Look carefully at a torch bulb or a clear glass light bulb when it is not lit up.

Two metal posts stick up from the base inside the light bulb.

A very thin wire runs between them. It is called the filament. The filament is made of a metal which can get very hot without melting.

All the light comes from this filament.

The electricity runs up inside one metal post, through the filament and back down the other post.

The filament is so thin that the electricity has to push hard to get through.

The pushing makes the filament heat up. The filament gets so hot that it glows brightly and gives out light.

Do not look at the filament when light is coming from it. It is so bright that it could hurt your eyes.

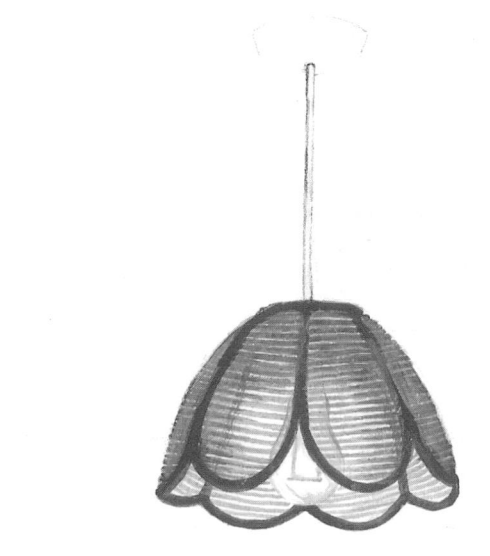

Look at all the light bulbs in
your house. How many
different sorts can you find?

Some light bulbs are made of
cloudy glass so that the light
does not dazzle you.

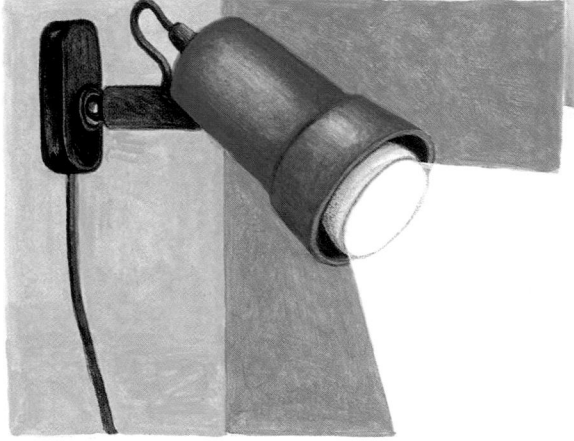

Spotlight bulbs are partly
coated with silver paint.
The light does not shine out
all round. It comes out
in one strong beam.

Strip lights do not have a
filament. The long thin tubes
are filled with gas. There is a
special coating on the inside
of the glass. As electricity
passes through the gas, the
coating glows and gives out a
strong white light. Strip lights
use less electricity than light
bulbs.

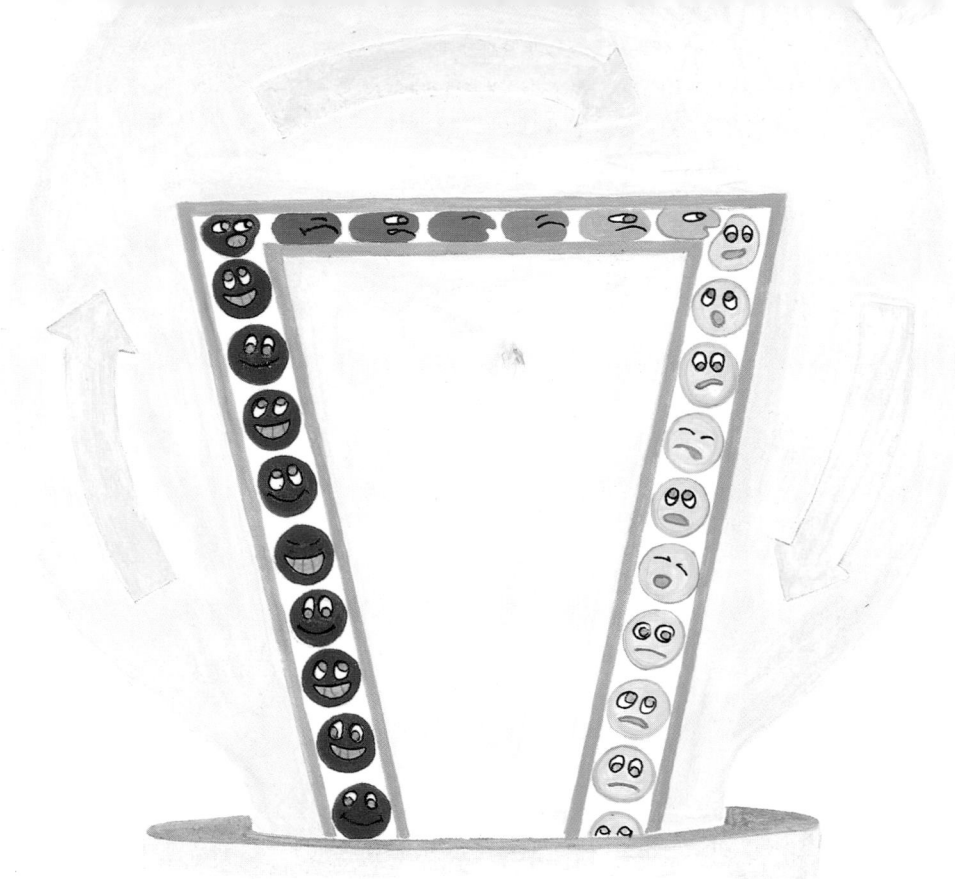

When electricity comes to your house it has the energy to do a lot of work. When electricity works hard it uses up its energy.

Electricity does not use up much energy flowing through the wire to the bulb. It uses up a lot of energy pushing through the filament.

When electricity flows away from the light, it has almost no energy left.

11

Making a Circuit

There are always two wires to a bulb because electricity cannot come and go along the same wire. It has to travel round a circuit.

A circuit is a one-way system without any gaps. Try making a circuit to light a torch bulb. (You will need a 4.5 volt battery bulb with a 4.5 volt battery.)

4.5v

1. Use a battery like this with metal strips on the top. These are called the terminals.

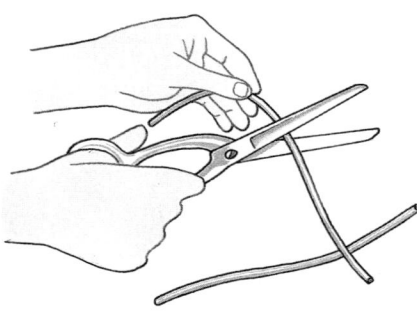

2. Cut two lengths of thin wire.

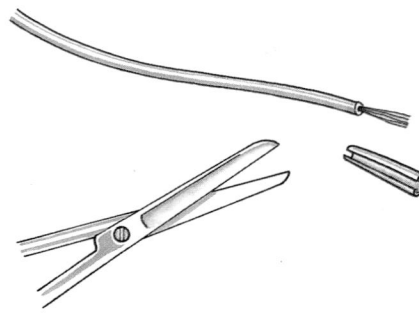

3. Cut the plastic away from the ends.

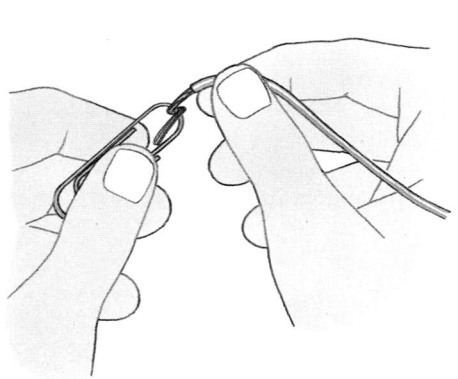

4. Twist the ends of each wire round paperclips (or fix them into crocodile clips).

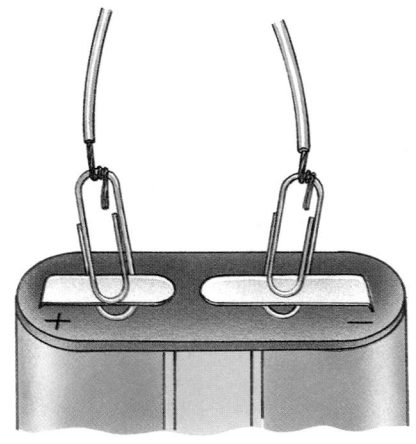

5. Clip a wire to each terminal.

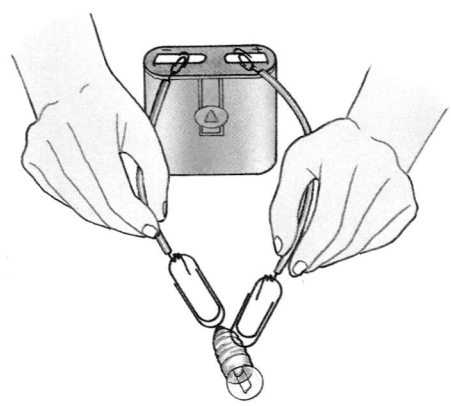

6. Touch a torch bulb with the other ends of the wires. Can you make it light up?

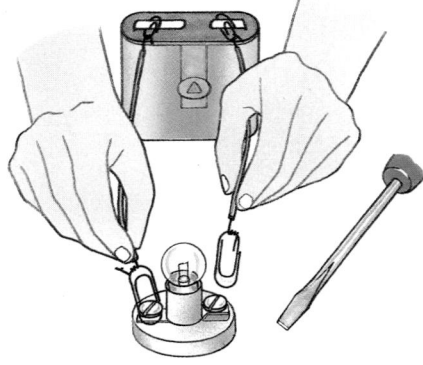

7. Screw the bulb into a bulb-holder. Can you make the bulb light up now?

Electricity can flow from one piece of metal to another if the pieces of metal are touching.

Look at the metal bumps on the base of a light bulb. They are connected to the filament.

Inside the bulb-holder there are two metal rods. They are connected to the ends of the wires.

When the light bulb is fitted into the bulb-holder, the metal parts touch. Electricity can now flow into the bulb and out again.

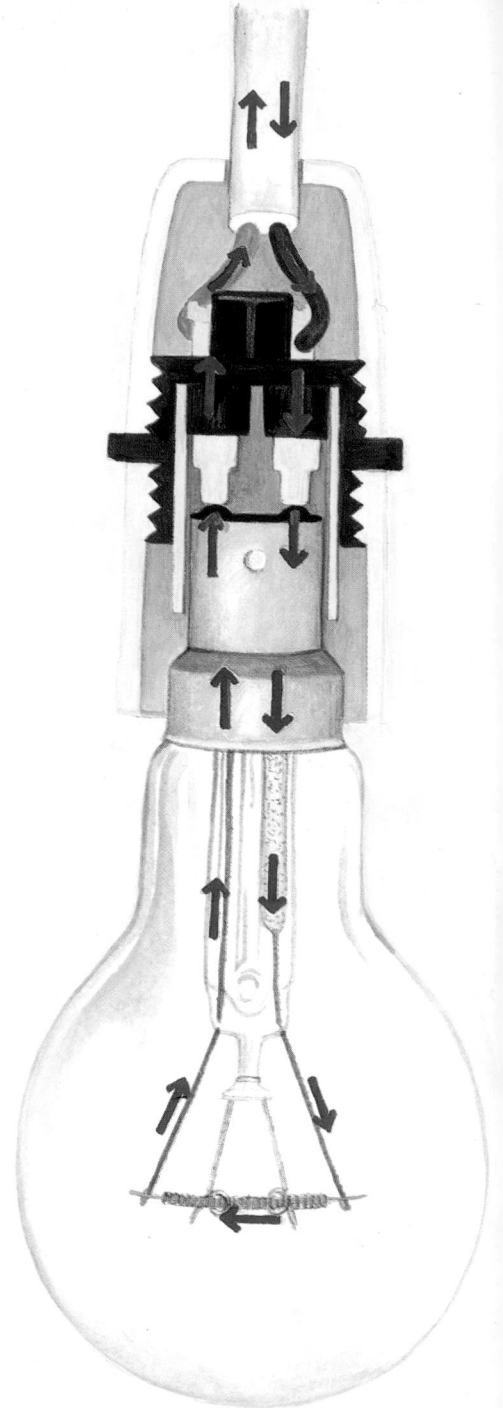

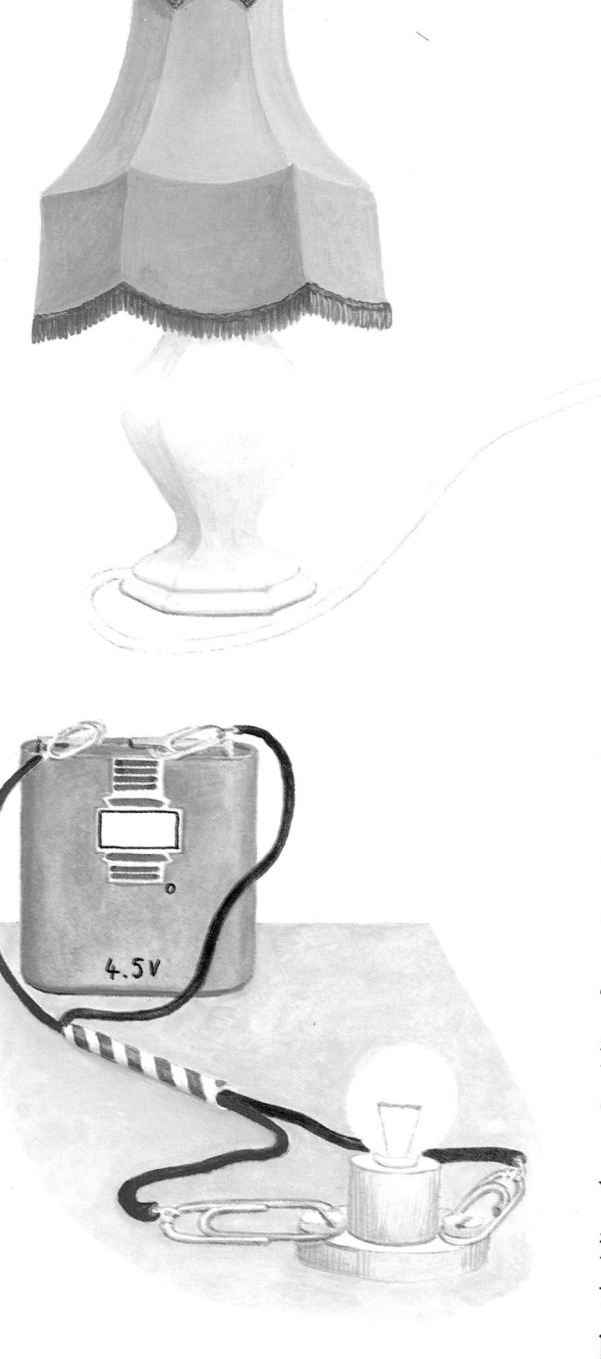

All lights need one wire for electricity to come along and another wire to pass it away.

This light looks as if it only has one wire. It is called a flex. Inside the flex there are separate wires.

The wires are kept together in one flex to protect them and keep them tidy.

You can keep the wires in your circuit together by threading them through a plastic straw.

Flexes and Wires

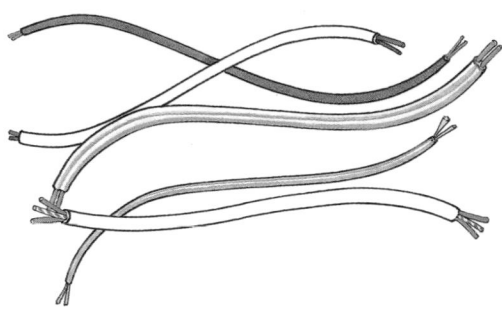

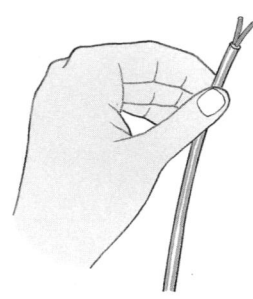

1. Make a collection of old pieces of flex which are not attached to anything.

2. Look at the wires inside each piece. The colours tell you the jobs they do.

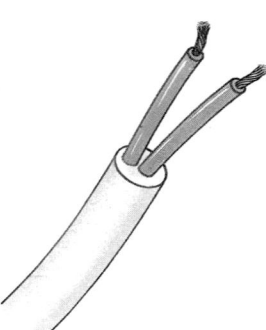

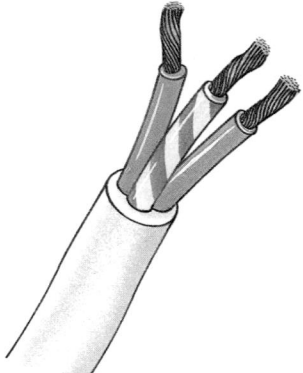

3. The flex to a light usually has two wires, coloured brown and blue. The brown wire is called the live wire. It carries electricity which has lots of energy. The blue wire is called the neutral wire. It carries away electricity which has lost most of its energy.

4. Flex which carries a lot of electricity may also contain a stripy green and yellow wire. It is called the earth wire. If electricity escapes, it can be very dangerous. The earth wire can let it flow safely away down into the earth.

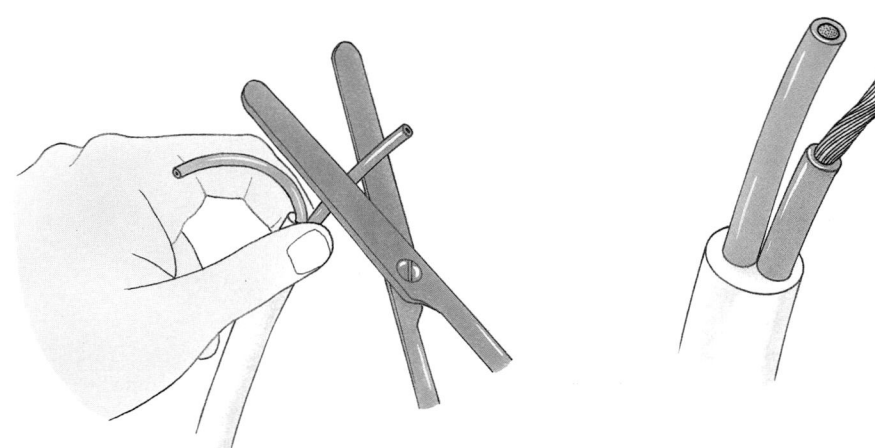

5. Cut the plastic away from the ends of some wires to look at the metal inside.

6. Electric wire is usually made of copper. Copper lets electricity through very easily.

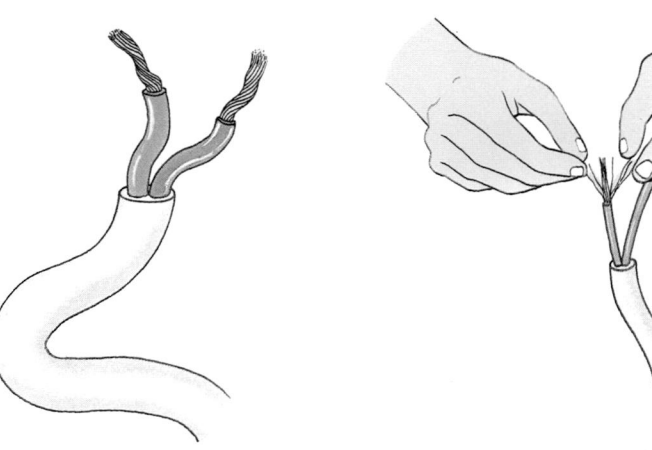

7. The flex is bendy because the wires are made of lots of thin strands. Solid wire would not bend.

8. Count the strands in each wire. Wires which carry a lot of electricity need a lot of strands to do the job.

If you touched a bare wire which had electricity running through it, the electricity would flow through you to the ground. It would give you an electric shock and could kill you.

Electricity cannot pass through plastic, so plastic keeps the electricity flowing safely along inside the wire.

The wires are covered with plastic for safety.

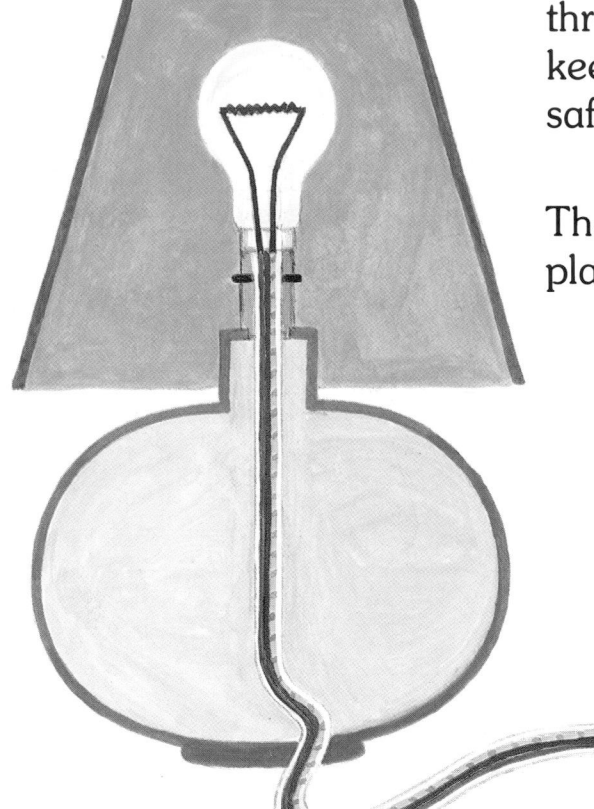

What Can Electricity Flow Through?

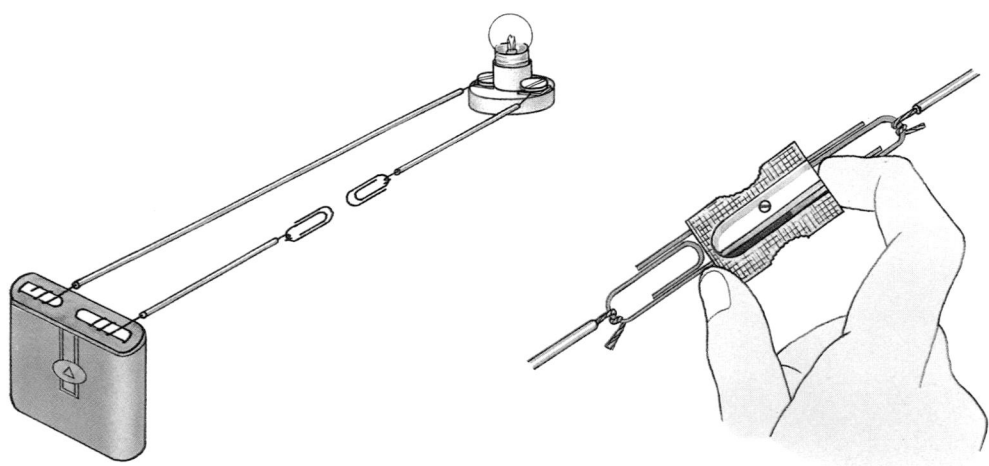

1. Make a circuit like this with one long and two short wires. Leave a gap between the paperclips on the ends of the short wires.

2. Collect objects made of different materials, such as metal, plastic and cloth. Try bridging the gap with each object.

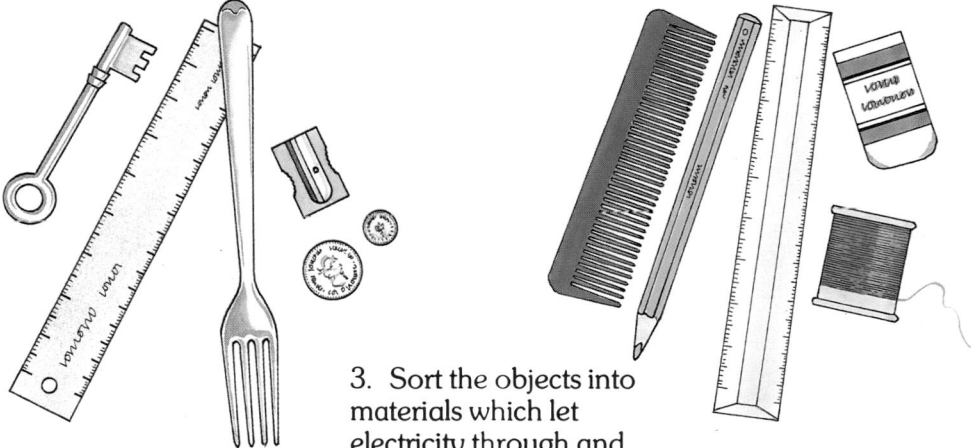

3. Sort the objects into materials which let electricity through and materials which do not.

Materials which let electricity through are called conductors. Most metals are conductors.

Materials which do not let electricity through are called insulators. Plastic is an insulator.

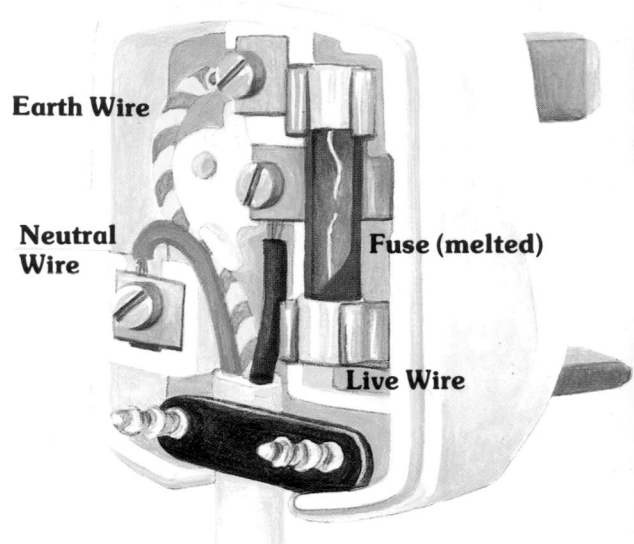

Earth Wire

Neutral Wire

Fuse (melted)

Live Wire

There is a plug on the end of this flex. It fits into a socket on the wall.

Each wire in the flex must be connected to the right prong inside the plug.

There is a fuse in the plug. The fuse is like a little barrel with a thin wire inside.

Electricity comes through the fuse before it reaches the live wire.

If too much electricity flows into the wire the fuse wire heats up and melts. The electricity cannot cross the gap and reach the live wire.

The plug has metal prongs which fit into matching holes in the socket. When the socket is switched on, the prongs are connected up to the ends of wires behind the wall.

Electricity flows from the live wire behind the wall into the live wire in the plug.

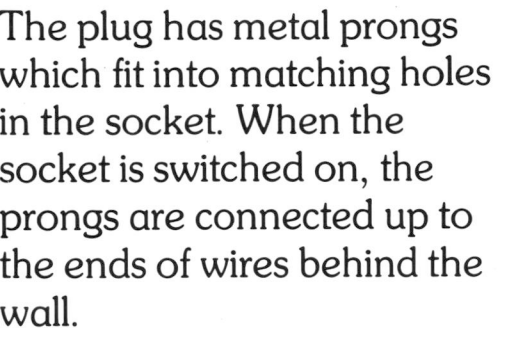

Do not play with sockets because the electricity is ready waiting to flow out.

When you turn a switch off, the back part
tilts and pushes two pieces of metal apart.

This makes a gap in the wire. The electricity
stops flowing and the bulb goes out.

When you turn the switch on,
the pieces of metal spring
together again. Electricity
flows through and lights the
bulb.

Make a Switch

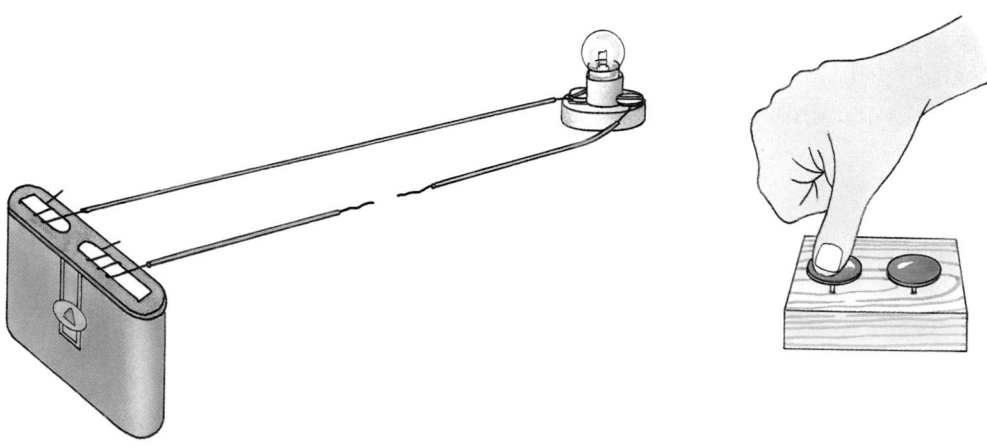

1. Make a circuit like this with a gap on one side.

2. Press small drawing pins into a piece of soft wood (or use split pins on card).

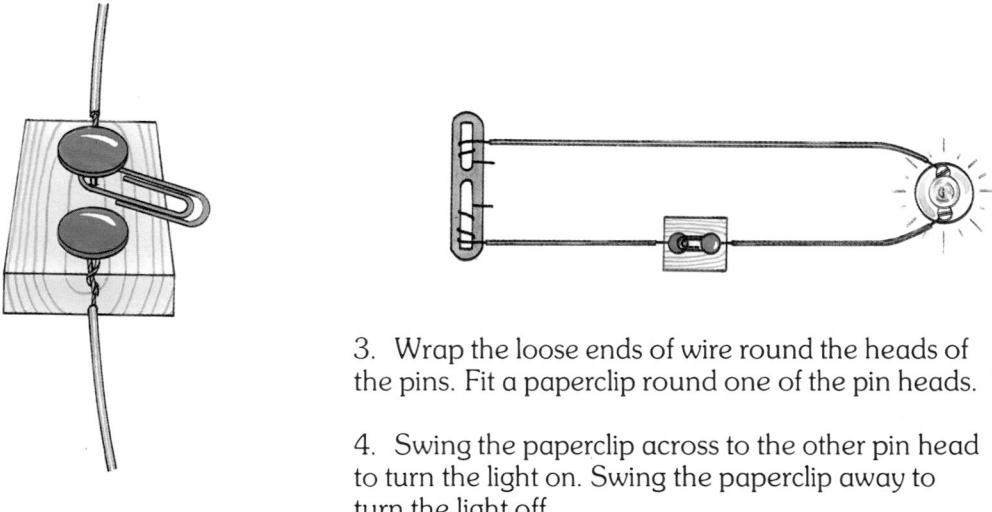

3. Wrap the loose ends of wire round the heads of the pins. Fit a paperclip round one of the pin heads.

4. Swing the paperclip across to the other pin head to turn the light on. Swing the paperclip away to turn the light off.

In most rooms there are lights fixed to the ceiling.

The switch is placed where it is easy to reach. It may be a long way from the light.

Wires are laid behind the wall. The live wire branches off to go to the switch.

The wires travel up and across the ceiling. They come down through a hole in the plaster.

There is a cover over the hole called a ceiling rose. Inside the rose, the wires from above the ceiling join up with wires in the flex to the light.

Make a Ceiling Light

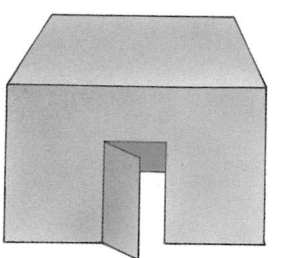

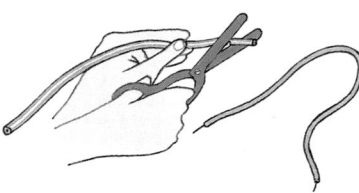

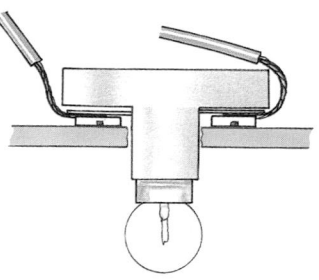

1. Make a room from a cardboard box. Cut a door in one side.

2. Cut two long wires like this.

3. Fix the ends to a bulb-holder and fit the light through the ceiling.

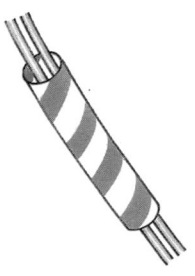

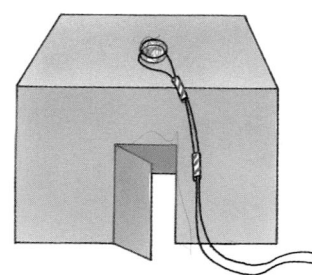

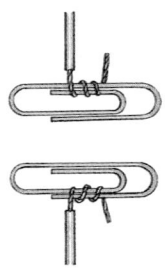

4. Slip rings of plastic straw over the wires to hold them together.

5. Bring the wires over the top of the ceiling and down by the door.

6. Cut one of the wires and fix paperclips to the metal.

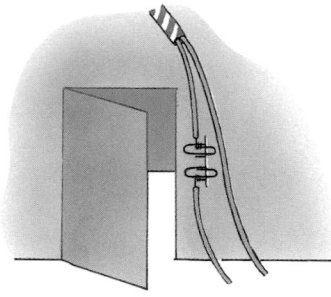

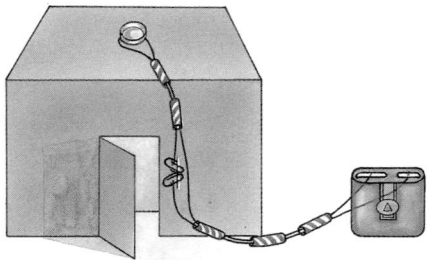

7. Cut slits in the cardboard to fasten the paperclips to the wall to make a switch.

8. Attach the wire ends to the battery. Work the switch by moving the paperclips on the wall together and apart.

Electricity flows around the house through cables which are usually hidden out of sight.

Cable is thicker and stronger than flex. It does not bend as easily.

A ring of cable runs around the house to connect up the lights. Another ring of cable connects up the sockets.

▶ This cable contains a red live wire, a black neutral wire and an earth wire for safety.

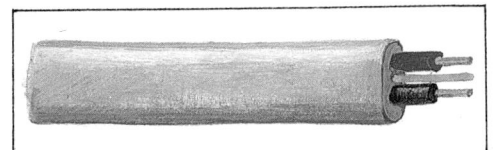

The cables for each circuit start from a control panel in your house.

Cables for all the circuits set off from the control panel like railway lines leaving a station.

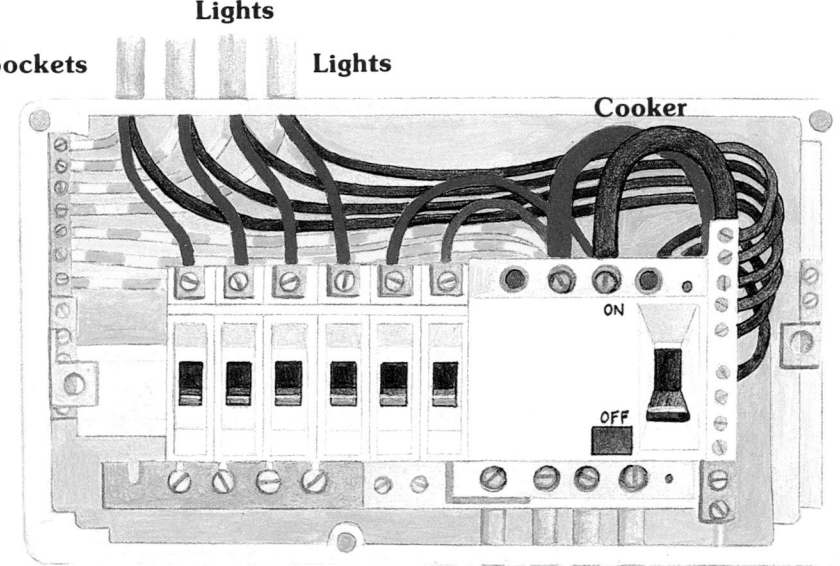

Sockets

Lights

Lights

Cooker

ON

OFF

On the control panel you can see a box which contains the mains switch. If the mains switch is turned off, no electricity can flow round the house.

Near the mains switch there is a row of fuses or circuit breakers. There is one fuse to protect each circuit in the house.

The cables are not all the same size. The cooker needs a thicker cable than the lights because it uses more electricity.

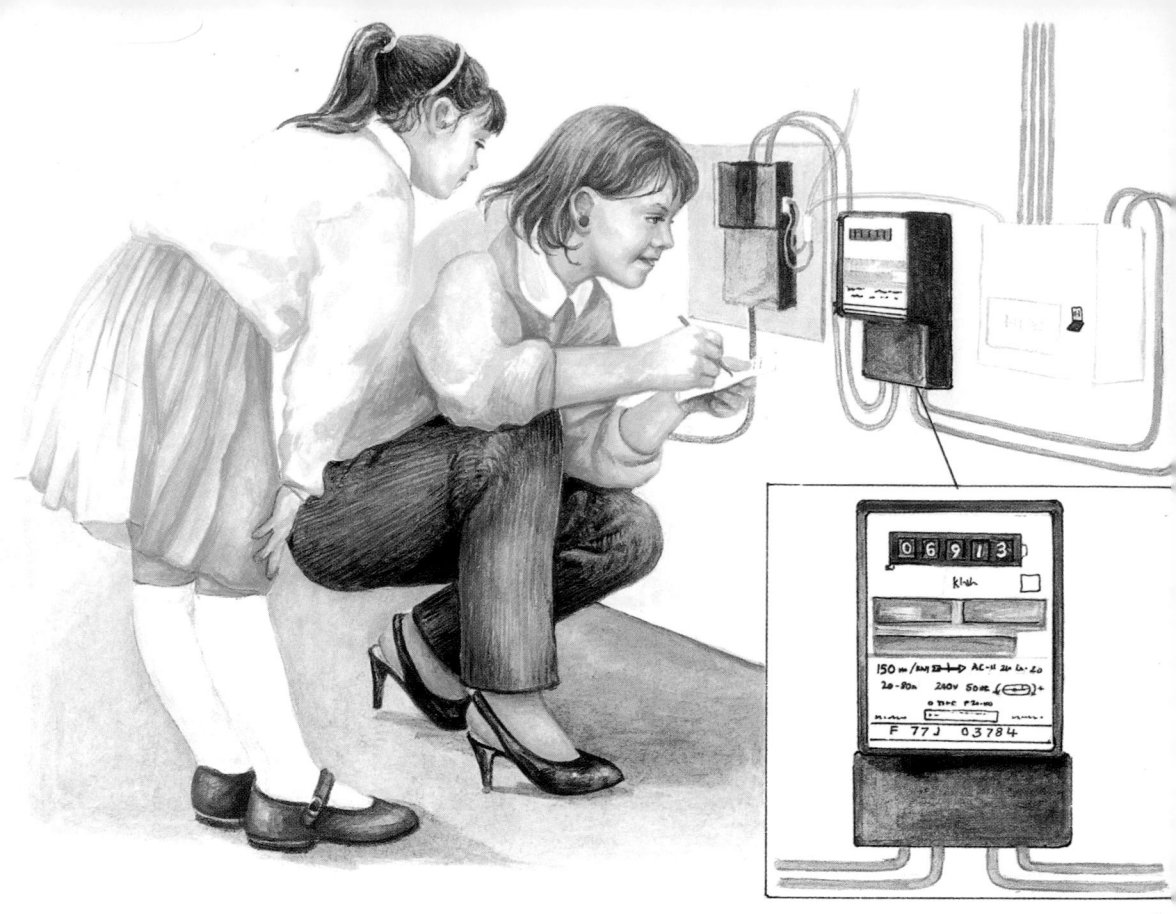

The electricity which flows into your house passes through an electricity meter before it reaches the mains switch.

The meter shows how many units of electricity have been used and will have to be paid for.

Look at the meter in your house. Some meters have a clock dial for each of the numbers. Some meters count the units with digital numbers. Some meters count daytime and night-time units separately. Electricity costs less at night.

An electric fire takes about half an hour to use one whole unit of electricity. A light bulb takes much longer.

Light bulbs may be marked 25 w, 40 w, 60 w, 100 w or 150 w.

W stands for watts. A 100 watt bulb is brighter than a 60 watt bulb.

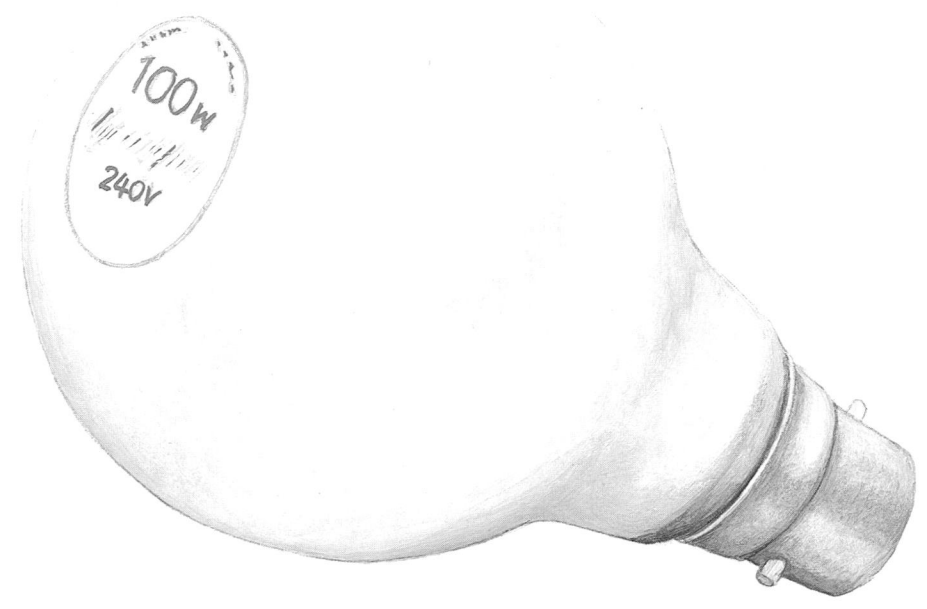

A 100 watt bulb takes ten hours to use a unit of electricity. A 60 watt bulb takes longer.

Look for the markings on light bulbs in your house.

Mains electricity comes from power stations.

A boiler heats up water to make steam. The steam drives engines called turbines which spin huge electromagnets.

The electromagnets generate electricity inside coils of wire. They push the electrons which are tiny bits in the wire. This starts a wave of energy flowing along the wire.

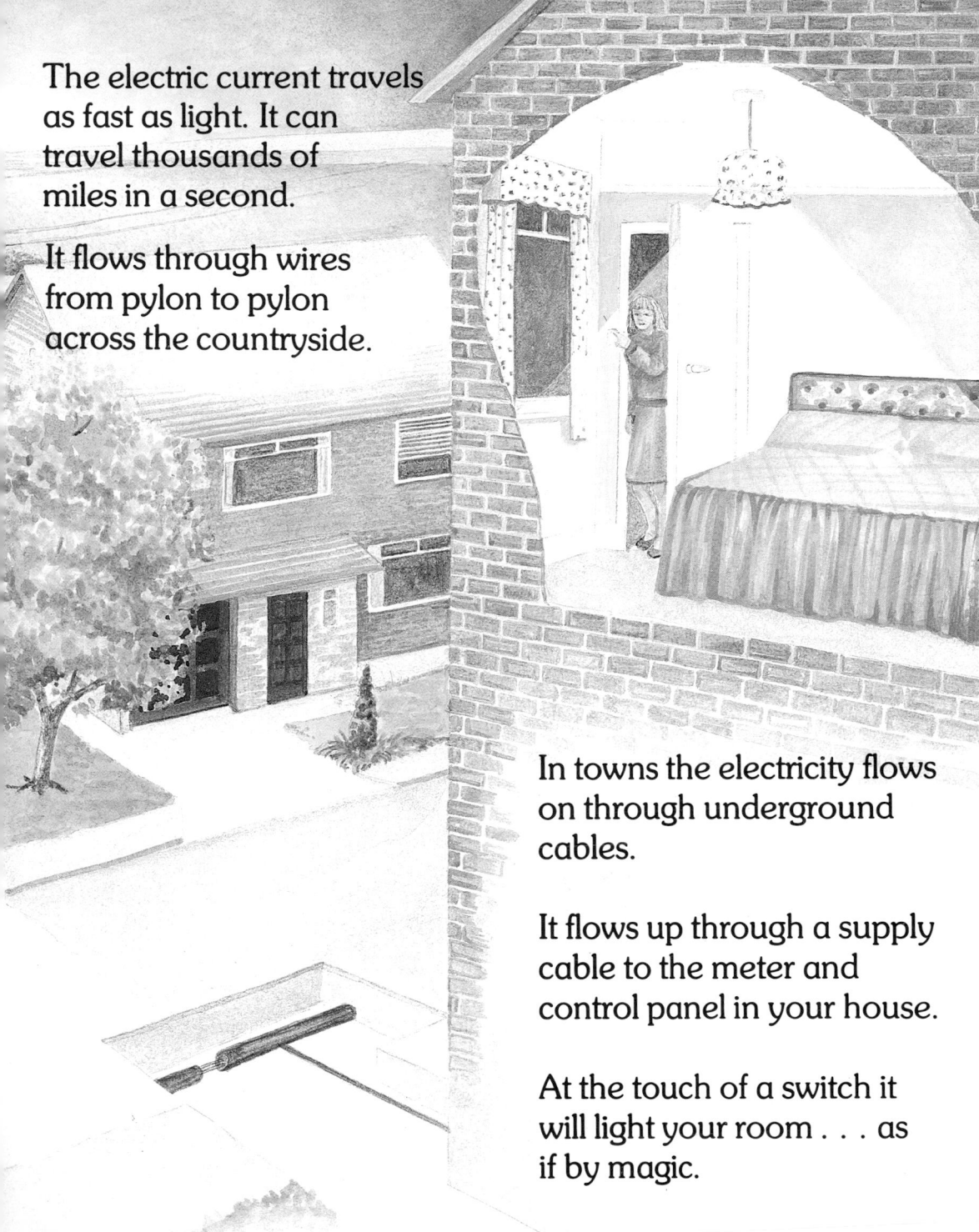

The electric current travels as fast as light. It can travel thousands of miles in a second.

It flows through wires from pylon to pylon across the countryside.

In towns the electricity flows on through underground cables.

It flows up through a supply cable to the meter and control panel in your house.

At the touch of a switch it will light your room . . . as if by magic.

INDEX

 PRINTED IN BELGIUM BY
proost
INTERNATIONAL BOOK PRODUCTION